Beauty and the Beads

A Short Erotic Weight Gain Tale of Two BBW Lesbians

By Molly Weisser

DEDICATION

To all who share in the pleasure and affirmation in erotic weight gain kink community.

DESCRIPTION

Kaydee, a super-size professional jeweler living in rural New Mexico, is incredibly lonely. But one day, a pretty plump girl named Lindsay wanders into her shop enthusing about history. Kaydee, her hunger for companionship too strong to resist, devises a plan to kidnap Lindsay and force her to balloon up. This power struggle takes an unexpected turn, however, when Lindsay's resistance becomes unrepentant gluttony – for food, and for love.

This story is a quasi-realistic piece of lesbian BBW erotic weight gain fiction involving the following elements:
NONCONSENSUAL gaining, Magical Pharmaceuticals, Extreme weight gain (200lbs+), Feeder/feedee relationship, Belly play (slapping, jiggling, etc.), Boob/moob play (slapping, jiggling, etc.), Ropes, Extreme weight gain (200lbs+). A modern-day lesbian BBW/BBW romance with food fetishization and weight-gain kinkiness. Written as a commission for D.M. and published with permission.

BEAUTY AND THE BEADS

The chakra bells on the front door jangled, causing Kaydee to open one lazy eye. After the Valentine's day rush, her store -- Earth, Wind, and Laughter – generally went ignored.

The merchants of Shaynaschee, New Mexico generally didn't get a lot of sales mid-winter. Maybe a few snowbirds straying from Santa Fe would pop in and buy a few trinkets for their grandkids, but that was about it.

Kaydee was one of the lucky ones, who had enough business savvy to keep her Yelp page updated, her TripAdvisor page current, and her Facebook page auto-posting whatever she photographed for Instagram. She also had the advantage of having a very interesting storefront and advertisements posted on the main highway.

And still, a serious customer the day before March began was practically unheard of.

But she shouldn't act too curious. Kaydee didn't want to scare off the shiny-eyed white woman standing in the doorway, looking as timid as a fawn.

"Hello," the woman asked, while Kaydee did her best to look bored, "are you open?"

Kaydee opened her eyes and squinted at the customer. The woman in front of her – practically just a girl, really – was wearing a magenta wool coat, tight jade leggings that seemed to be plastered to her thighs, and a bright yellow sweater. This latter did very little to flatter an exceptionally plump tummy that overhung the waistband of her pants. The tiniest crescent-moon of skin peeked out from beneath the fabric, making Kaydee's mouth water with urgent desire.

A flash of insight streaked across Kaydee's mind, and she instantaneously imagined the woman prostrate on her sagging bed, nakedly exposed for Kaydee's delectation.

She closed her eyes and took a deep breath. How likely was it that a willing subject for her perverse fantasies would wander their way through her door? Certainly not in this lifetime.

So, Kaydee just sighed and wiped the crumbs of her eleven-o'clock snack off her large, soft belly. For the millionth time recently, Kaydee contemplated upon how lonely she was.

. . . .

The summer tourist season had been a good one, at least. Kaydee had gotten rounder, filled to the brim with happy foods purchased with luscious green dollars. The imminent future lean times were visible on the horizon, true, but for the moment she could still luxuriate in the knowledge that her expenses were paid for the winter, and she could simply eat the rest of her money away with impunity.

Of course, the problem with Kaydee's well-lined pockets was that her physical port was also growing. Her six-XL dresses were getting snug on her petite frame, and she was long past squareness of dimensions. She was sixty-three inches tall, sixty-six inches from side to side, and over two hundred inches around the widest point of her belly.

Over the course of the year, usually her weight rose and fell within the range of six hundred to six hundred and forty, but this winter she was nearing the tipping point of six hundred and fifty pounds. It was an awesome, powerful, and terrifying number, resulting in simultaneous fascination and horror that led to an almost magical reverence.

She'd wait to weigh herself, scared to see if she'd crossed that all-important number. Then she would finally cave in the middle of the night when out of erotically-powered insomnia, she'd gorged herself to bursting. Thus armed, she would boldly get upon her talking scale, and then sigh with mixed relief and self-loathing as the announcement came: she was still in the forties.

All of this was moot, however, once dawn came and roused her from the sweat-ridden sheets of her overtaxed bed: No one wanted to be with a woman as large as her.

. . . .

Not that she hadn't been trying, of course. She didn't expect someone from high school to profess their undying love for her salty ass over Facebook. She didn't expect a prince or princess charming to sweep her off her feet. And she didn't expect that she wouldn't have to make compromises: as she jokingly told friends, she figured that of the trifecta of looks, brains, and money, she'd have to pick at most two, and possibly settle for one.

Yeah, she'd done the typical things that a single person looking for a date would do. She'd done dating apps. She'd done matchmakers. She'd done internet chatrooms. She'd done bars. And while she had not-entirely-unfavorable results in the sexual adventuring department, when it came to actual love and shit, she hadn't had any real bites in years.

More fish in the sea? Bah. Kaydee was over that. She knew there were no more fish to be found. All the men who liked her were creeps, all the women who liked her were one-night stands who hated themselves in the morning, and everyone in between wanted nothing to do with her at all. She'd been doing this long enough that Kaydee knew the next time she let her heart be broken by a pretty face who wouldn't call back, she wouldn't be able to do it again.

The most recent time was the most painful one, actually. She'd found this girl – Zilly - on a dating forum for plus-size folks.

At first they were victim to the terrible type of chit-chat that predominates such dating apps. "Hello," "How are you," "What's up?" "Nothing much what's up with you" and so forth.

But they escaped that mire when Kaydee mentioned her jewelry business, and learned Zilly had formerly been a 'sales consultant' for a shitty jewelry company but learned more about the business and got out without too big a loss. Cementing their mutual interest, they talked endlessly about their experiences with various multilevel marketing hacks, which quality of silver was actually worth the price, and gripes about self-employment taxes.

And then, their casual chit-chat led to flirting. Their flirting led to long phone conversations at night for months and months. Their long conversations at night led to a date in Santa Fe, around a hundred miles from Kaydee's home.

The spark they'd had from a distance? Kaydee thought it held up to the harsh light of reality. The way Zilly smiled at her, the way Zilly pushed more cheesecake on Kaydee's plate, and the way that Zilly chattered away eagerly while Kaydee munched and munched… all of this led Kaydee to assume the best.

Returning home again, she was on cloud nine, and she talked endlessly about Zilly to anyone who would listen.

But it seems the feeling was not mutual. Or at least, something changed, because Kaydee's texts started to go unanswered. Kaydee tried to be chipper, but her mood turned darker and more sour. And then, as her heart slowly began to bleed itself dry, Zilly answered!

But instead of the unrepentant friendliness that Zilly displayed prior to the trip, Kaydee found Zilly to be all seriousness. unwinding all the reasons she couldn't date Kaydee.

It was mostly bullshit reasons. But Kaydee held onto every single word Zilly said.

Kaydee was too needy.

Kaydee wanted too much too soon.

Kaydee's relationship pace was out of sync with this other person.

Kaydee caused this person anxiety for not being good enough.

And ultimately, Kaydee's desires were too intense.

It was this final thing that broke Kaydee's spirit the most, for Kaydee had, during those long phone conversations at night, revealed things to Zilly that she'd never revealed before. Things that, in truth, frightened her. Things that, she was certain, were the real reason Zilly had stopped answering her messages.

Things that she'd locked up in a vault so tight, she would never dare share them again.

. . . .

Now, in the present moment, it felt as if her brain was about to burst. The intense longing of her heart combined with the serious pressure growing in her lower regions, and the noxious chemical haze of lust began to filter through her body.

Not that this customer would ever know, of course. Kaydee was pretty good at hiding her feelings, especially in a sales context.

The other woman's hazel eyes were engaged in looking across the jewelry on offer, roaming with a preciseness and deliberateness that reminded Kaydee of a hawk surveying the desert mountains. Kaydee, for her part, sat with her plump beringed hands folded upon her massive stomach, and she was pretending to watch the television that posed next to her empty pizza box.

Finally, after a few intense moments, Kaydee was startled to realize that the customer was pointing at one particular pendant in the lighted glass cabinet.

A pricey one, too. A valuable antique bone and shell clasp from the late Georgian period. It wasn't much to look at, but worth more than its weight in gold due to its age and history.

"That looks old," the customer offered, and grinned. "You got some good stuff, here."

Kaydee rumbled comfortably and readjusted herself in her seat. "We do our best to intrigue our customers," she said, though the 'we' was an affectation. Her typical sales spiel was that she was Laughter, and that her partners Earth and Wind were busy at the moment.

No need to mention that the Earth and Wind she referred to were the literal Earth and Wind.

Usually no one gave a crap about it, but for some reason this woman looked curious.

"You have a husband?" asked the customer, her light long brown hair bobbing.

"Never," Kaydee said, in what could best be described as 'a hiss,' but she realized her miscalculation quickly. "I mean, I don't think I could actually marry a man. Such pigs."

She guessed from the woman's rainbow clutch that the words would fall on receptive ears, and Kaydee was gratified to see the customer nod.

"But if you're so inclined," Kaydee went on, warming to her topic, "I'm sure you'd have picked a nice one who would deserve something like… like this tie pin."

She reached in front of her for her pointing wand, and she extended it across the glass counter to tap above the item in question.

To be honest, this was a test of the woman's ignorance. The tie pin was overpriced rubbish from a thrift store that Kaydee had dressed up with her refurbishment tools. But the credulous customer could be tempted with the right story.

Indeed, this girl seemed just the type to fall for a tall tale. She nodded along patiently, eyes wide and eager, and she smiled as Kaydee's eyes met her own.

"I got this pin from an old veteran," Kaydee elaborated, leaning forward with effort. "He used to be in the U.S. Marine Corps, and he sold it to me to finance a down-payment for his daughter's new house. It was a treasured memento from the Vietnam years. He said that LBJ himself was taking a shower at Camp David. And while there, Richard Nixon barged on into the bathroom in a frenzied state before anyone could stop him. There was yelling at first, but then they calmed down and were talking. While the veteran didn't know exactly what went down, when Nixon left the bathroom, Johnson was saying, 'Fine, Dick, fine. You'll get what you want, don't you worry. Enjoy it.' And then a few days later, Johnson announced he would not be running for re-election!"

To top off the story, Kaydee added with a flourish, "And as he was leaving the bathroom? Johnson was carrying his dirty clothes, including this tie pin, which he dropped."

The woman squinted hard at Kaydee, and then laughed. "That's a good story," she said, and grinned. "I find it hard to believe, though."

"No, no, don't take my word for it!" Kaydee said, adding the piece-de-resistance. "Take a look at the pin." So saying, she withdrew a key from her key ring, and opened the glass case.

Then she picked up the pin, and turned it over under the glass, letting it shine in the light.

Visibly, the customer breathed in a gasp as she saw the initials engraved on the pin: LBJ.

In reality, the pin likely predated the Vietnam War, garbage from the 40s or something, but the impact of the indisputable proof of the story seemed to sink in.

"Oooh," the customer said, and her eyes opened wide. "That's spooky. I don't even care if the story is true or not, I am convinced."

Kaydee preened. "Everything in here has a story. You just got to know how to listen to it."

While this could have been seen as an admission of having made up the tale about the pin, the customer did not seem to suspect anything.

"That's so cool," the girl said, and smiled. "My name is Lindsay, by the way."

"Kaydee Brown," answered the jeweler coolly, but her eyes were calculating as she looked Lindsay up and down. "I haven't seen you around town before. It's not a big place, Shaynaschee."

"No, it's not," agreed Lindsay cordially. "I'm here on a short term research fellowship for the state of New Mexico. I have what we historians call 'special dispensation' to review the town records. I'm here to digitize everything Shaynaschee has and codify it for future review."

"Probably not too much in the way of records," Kaydee observed, "seeing the town is so small."

"Well that's where it gets interesting," Lindsay enthused, and she leaned against the counter. Ordinarily Kaydee would have shaken her head disapprovingly at this kind of thing, but she couldn't help but like this funny woman in bright clothes who had wandered into her shop this morning. She was willing to hear the woman out.

Not to mention, the view from her end was extraordinary, while Lindsay leaned against the counter. Cleavage farther than the eyes could track! It was thrilling to let the eye wander into the dark place between her perky white breasts and ponder the depths of her deliciousness.

Quite frankly, it stirred up Kaydee's lust again – dreadfully bad.

"There was a community of Latter-Day Saints that used to live on the town's outskirts," Lindsay gushed, and she used her pudgy fingers to draw upon the glass case. "And perhaps you know, the LDS community is pretty damn good at keeping records. Proving direct lineage to Joseph Smith and so forth."

Kaydee hated fingerprints on her glass case, but the temptations of Lindsay's breasts fascinated her, so much so that she couldn't get the words together to admonish the customer. They heaved with every excited breath Lindsay made, and Kaydee couldn't help but imagine what it would be like to make Lindsay gasp like that her own damn self, out of fierce erotic desire and stimulation…

"So eventually the church moved on," Lindsay continued, gazing at the ceiling and oblivious to Kaydee's wandering eyes, "and eventually what happened is they ceded the records to the city library. I guess they intended that to be a temporary move, but that was around fifty years ago. So they officially belong to the city archives."

She paused, gasping for breaths after this long and dramatically-delivered monologue, and Kaydee realized that she might be waiting for an answer.

"Meaning that the city archives are far more vast than passersby of this little town would suspect," Kaydee said, hoping to keep Lindsay talking.

Yes, indeed. She was really, really enjoying this little diversion. It was the closest she'd gotten to being turned on by someone in real life in a long time. And so she decided: she would prolong it as much as possible.

After around an hour of chatting, Lindsay left, her sumptuous bubbly butt twerking with every step. And even though she hadn't made a purchase, Kaydee felt more satisfied than she'd felt in a long fucking time.

She went to bed very, very early that night.

. . . .

Kaydee, while deeply attracted to Lindsay's spirit and essence, was also secretly ridden with desire for Lindsay's potential.

Potential for Lindsay's wobbly, rubbery tummy to soften until it spilled out like melting butter across her thighs when she sat.

Potential for Lindsay's dimpled, succulent thighs to ripen into overstuffed cushions of padding to hide Lindsay's fat little cunt.

Potential for Lindsay's pubic fat to rise from that cute cupcake-sized camel-toe into a truly delectable cake of moist deliciousness, as large as a melon.

Potential for Lindsay's melon-sized breasts to inflate to the size of smooth beach balls, bouncing joyously with every wonderful gasping breath she took.

Potential for Lindsay's whole plump little body to enlarge: to grow beyond its current delightful parameters and become a rival in size to Kaydee's own.

These were sick thoughts, Kaydee knew, and depraved thoughts. But they were thoughts that had plagued her since an incredibly early age. Thoughts she kept shoving into that deep dark vault inside her. And every time that vault threatened to burst open, she just shoved more food inside her greedy mouth.

Oh god.

Kaydee couldn't stand it anymore. She fingered herself so vigorously, jiggling every ounce of lard on her pubic area, her mind wandering over the body of her imaginary Lindsay. Her stomach rumbled with hunger, a hunger deeper than her stomach, and she pierced the ceiling of her vagina with expert fingers.

If only…

If only…

Oh god!!!

. . . .

Kaydee never expected to see Lindsay again in her life, but was delighted to see the woman popped back in the next day. Lindsay had a sandwich with her – one that Kaydee approved of, a twelve-inch sub with an exorbitant amount of ham, cheese, and salami.

"Hey," Lindsay said, looking shy. "I'm on lunch, and I really enjoyed our talk yesterday. You mind if I eat my lunch here?"

Kaydee, flabbergasted, agreed, and joked. "Of course. But I hope you brought me something."

"Funny you should say that," Lindsay said, and smiled. "I do happen to have an extra one."

And, to Kaydee's surprise, Lindsay produced a second, identical sandwich.

"You… you seem like someone who likes to eat?" Lindsay asked, and heaven help her, did she blush?

"No," Kaydee said, and initially pushed away the sandwich. The girl looked crestfallen, until Kaydee reached down to her handy condiment shelf and revealed some mustard. "I love to eat."

Lindsay laughed, though it seemed somewhat forced – clearly she was expecting rejection, and Kaydee's mean streak had hit uncomfortably hard.

To apologize, Kaydee was happy to find a home for that whole damn sandwich in her gut, even though she'd polished off an unusual amount of her breakfast casserole this morning. The cold cuts tasted all the sweeter and the bread tasted all the softer for the fact that they had been bought for her.

And, well, it actually made Kaydee have a glimmer of hope for the first time in a long while. Perhaps she had actually found someone who she could relate to, in a deep way.

. . . .

The week went by faster than any other week in Kaydee's life up until then. Lindsay would come in every day during her lunch period, bringing something delicious every time. Kaydee strove to do her part to find something new and exciting to share from her jewelry stash every day. But honestly, the food and the company were the features of the sessions.

As part of her experience, Kaydee carefully collected facts about Lindsay every day.

Fact: Lindsay looked adorable when mustard dripped down her double chins.

Fact: Lindsay loved eggplant parmigiana and ordered herself two.

Fact: When Lindsay ate chocolate chip cookies, she looked like a fat little chipmunk stuffing her cheeks.

Fact: Lindsay always ate too much at every meal, and would lean back in her chair and rub her tummy, oohing and ahhhing about how much she'd eaten.

Fact: Lindsay was very amused to learn about Kaydee's hourly meal schedule, and couldn't stop talking about how Kaydee would surely eat her 'out of house and home.' But she was smiling the whole time, almost admiringly.

Fact: Lindsay showed Kaydee a picture of what she'd looked like in high school, and it made heat immediately sink to her nethers.

"You were a high school cheerleader," Kaydee said, eyes wide. "With a body to match."

At Kaydee's evident surprise, Lindsay giggled. "I guess I must have mis-heard something my first year of college. Because I could swear that the saying was not 'the freshman fifteen' but 'the freshman fifty.'"

Kaydee was incredulous, but had also gained around fifty pounds her first year of college (though she'd started at a respectably larger size… around Lindsay's current size actually.) She'd never heard someone make that joke before, aside from her, and it simultaneously warmed her heart and something deeper inside her body.

As Lindsay was getting ready to go, Kaydee tried her best to express this, not willing to wait another second. She was ready to reveal her nighttime fantasies of enlarging Lindsay beyond average human proportions. Her sense that Lindsay was small, and needed to put in some effort to build up her body to where it would be truly satisfying as a lover to Kaydee. Her physical and mental hunger for food and the way they intersected with her lust. Her painful horniness aching in her panties, the wetness of her bedsheets this whole week, and the image at the forefront of her mind that she might satisfy Lindsay's every gustatory fancy and desire. The ingenious fattening plans she made upon Lindsay's plump person…

She couldn't bear keeping these things hidden anymore. Looking at Lindsay's bright and eager face, she knew in her heart of hearts that Lindsay would probably run straight away. But there was such a positive energy emanating from the other woman, Kaydee felt a powerful surge of hope… and she decided to take the chance.

"So, erm, Lindsay," Kaydee said, feeling her face heat up and sweat beginning to pool in her pits. "I… I have a question for you, if you don't mind."

Just then, though Lindsay's phone rang. She held up one pudgy finger, then answered it, mouthing the words, "it's my boss."

"Hey Saul," she said, her voice a little more high-pitched, betraying her nervousness. "How was your trip to Detroit?"

Then, with a wave goodbye, Lindsay walked out of the store, the chakra bells ringing behind her, and Kaydee's tongue burning.

. . . .

The next day, Kaydee was eager to see if Lindsay would return. She even went through her storage closet and found a lace tablecloth and a vase with silk flowers, so they could have a nicer environment for lunch.

But Lindsay's lunch period came and went, without a sign of the young woman. This left Kaydee feeling devastated. Of course this was just another failure to connect, same as the Zilly situation. And Kaydee? Well, she was writhing like a devil had gotten into her soul.

She closed the shop that day, not wanting to risk a customer coming in when she was in a foul mood. She lay on her poor over-worked bed, which strained to keep her massive body above the floor, and she cried.

She cried, in part, for Zilly – since this new exposure had re-opened that poorly-healed wound. But mostly she cried for having allowed herself to yet again be duped into having hopes and dreams.

And then, her mourning turned to anger – how dare people treat her so shabbily. And for what? If only Zilly had stayed, then Kaydee would have never had to think these thoughts again. Would never have fruitlessly prepared herself to be vulnerable. Would never have gotten herself wrapped up in the image of someone she thought she deserved.

How dare people make her feel so lonely?

Then. Then a truly bad, truly devious, almost evil idea came to her mind, unbidden. She could have everything she wanted: Lindsay; to not spend forever alone; to have the lovely and lusciously large partner of her dreams. All it would require would be a little work…

At first she tried to dismiss it, but the vault inside her heart that she'd been forcing closed… it wasn't closing no matter how much she pushed. It made her want to scream, and she knotted up her hands in her hair and she curled up into the sheets of her bed.

But then she grabbed her laptop, and started scrolling, reading, researching. And in that mixture of desperation, pain, and loneliness, a truly awful, depraved plan emerged.

She maxed out her credit cards that night, for the first time in her whole damn life.

…………………

The next day, a package was delivered. Kaydee lumbered out and took it from the carrier with a mixture of dread and cool fascination. As she tore it open with the box-cutter on her keychain, she almost couldn't believe what she'd done.

Thirty thousand dollars. She'd spent thirty thousand dollars on the internet last night, and twenty five thousand of those were in her hands right this moment. In a single little bottle.

Gransel Pharmaceuticals read the label, but it was a Korea-based company.

Twenty five thousand dollars on this bottle of fifty goddamn pills.

She desperately hoped that the reviews she'd read from her preferred feeder/feedee forums were going to prove correct. It'd be a fucking tragedy if she'd maxed out her credit on something useless.

Well, no time like the present to see if the things even worked.

She popped open the bottle with her thumb, and noticed that she was shaking. The pills were the color of pastel wedding pastilles, the size of Jordan almonds, and she was supposed to swallow them with water only.

Kaydee read the label, then trudged to the bathroom.

Six hundred and forty pounds, her scale announced in its cheerful, neutral robotic voice.

She stepped off the scale, then popped the pill, and drank the recommended four ounces of water.

There was an odd feeling in her body, like lead sinking in her stomach, but then that quickly went away, and she felt just a trifle heavier.

Maybe they had worked.

She stepped onto the scale again and held her breath.

Six hundred and fifty pounds the scale proclaimed.

Kaydee began to laugh giddily. Thanks to Gransel Pharmaceuticals, she had breached the six hundred and fifty pound mark, in less than one minute, and she hardly felt different at all.

This whole thing was going to be too, too easy.

But so much fucking fun.

. . . .

Feeling elated, Kaydee called down to the city library to inquire about Lindsay. The librarian assured Kaydee that Lindsay was called urgently back to Albuquerque and was bound to arrive back at work the next day.

This made Kaydee breathe a sigh of relief. The rest of the stuff she'd ordered hadn't all arrived yet, so she had some time to prepare. Not that she had any clue what on earth kind of work emergency a historian might have, but she at least understood it was a plausible reason. At least there seemed to be a somewhat reasonable explanation for her disappearance.

She left a message asking for Lindsay to call the store once she'd returned. And then she closed the store for the rest of the week.

. . . .

Lindsay did call the next day.

"Hey I'm so sorry for heading out of town without notice," she chirped, and Kaydee breathed a huge sigh of relief. "My boss had an emergency that needed some… management. But it's all fine now, so don't worry. I'm in the clear."

What a strange way to put it, but okay.

"That's great!" Kaydee declared, and keeping the buoyant tone of voice, she offered, "How about you come by after work on Friday? I got some really neat shipments in while you were away and I'm really excited to show them off."

"Neat, that works for me!" Lindsay said and Kaydee could tell the other woman was smiling. "I got to say, Kaydee, I really appreciate you. I was feeling so lonely in this town until I met you. It's nice to have a real friend I can trust."

It was a sweet sentiment, but Kaydee felt like a knife was twisting in her gut. But she bore through the pain, reminding herself that it all would be worth it, in the end. The ends justify the means. "I feel the same way," she said with a depth of feeling that probably didn't carry through the phone. "The same way."

They hung up after that, and Kaydee just grinned to herself. This chick had no clue what was coming.

. . . .

The plan after that was frighteningly simple.

#1. Convince Lindsay to come back to the store under any pretense necessary. Check.

#2. Once Lindsay let her guard down, chloroform. Check.

#3. Once Lindsay passed out, entrap her. Check.

#4. Once entrapped… feed.

Check, check, and check.

. . . .

"I don't understand," Lindsay whimpered. She was chained to the central support column of Kaydee's bedroom, handcuffed and also bound with ropes.

The ropes were not strictly necessary, but Kaydee had let her overwhelming sense of freedom and power dictate to what extent she bound her prisoner. Apparently, Kaydee really enjoyed playing with rope. Knotting it, wrapping it around plump wrists and ankles, braiding it into intricate macramé-style bindings around various places on Lindsay's fleshy places… oh yes, Kaydee loved this power.

The only thing Kaydee was wearing at this point was her own tightly-bound rope harness. It made her feel like an elf or fairy, to prance around in such a freeing costume that only accentuated the curves of her stomach, buttocks, and breasts. Her stomach swayed in a tantalizing manner, like a clock's pendulum, since every step she took required so much effort simply to move her heavy legs. And in particular, she adored the feelings of the knots she had tied up against her clit, which rubbed and stimulated her womanhood with every jiggle of her thighs.

"It's for your own good, sweetie," Kaydee cooed, and pressed a tender kiss upon Lindsay's soft brown head. "You are going to be mine, wholly and completely, darling. But I'm afraid I can't let you be free to move on your own. At least, not until you're too large to get yourself out that door."

She gestured to the entry to the bedroom that, with her breadth, was already a tight squeeze. It wasn't really what she intended, exactly – she liked the idea of Lindsay remaining a little bit smaller than her – but it had the dramatic effect she wanted.

"No," moaned Lindsay, her eyes wide. "Too big to get out of this room?"

"Oh yes, honey," Kaydee moaned in return, feeling her vagina squeeze in pre-orgasmic rapture. "You will be at least as big as me, dumpling."

"You can't make me," Lindsay breathed, clearly horrified. "I don't want to be… I don't want to…"

"Be fat?" asked Kaydee with glee. "Gargantuan? Gigantic? Oh, honey. No, no, you don't want to now. Of course not, my dear. I'm going to show you that I know what's best for you. And soon, you will be begging for me to feed you as much as your little belly can hold, and then some."

"No!" cried Lindsay, but followed this with the more demure, "No… no… no…"

"Chin up, darling," said Kaydee perkily, "I've spent a lot of money on you, dearheart, and I've got to have a good return on my investment. I am a businesswoman, you know."

"I… I thought you were my friend!" Lindsay sobbed, hanging her head and crying softly. "I can't believe you did this to me."

"Oh honey," Kaydee whispered, leaning towards Lindsay, letting her large, massive stomach with all its luxuriant rolls and folds press against the pudgy port of Lindsay's pot belly. "You're going to do this to yourself."

And so saying, before Lindsay knew what was happening, Kaydee popped one of the pastel pills into Lindsay's mouth, and Lindsay, frowning, swallowed it.

"What's this?" Lindsay asked, puzzled. "An antacid?"

"Of course, that's what it is," Kaydee said, and then pulled over a rolling cart stacked high with pizzas. "Now let's set about getting your belly nice and large for me, eh?"

Lindsay, while reluctant, obediently opened her mouth and allowed Kaydee to offer her pizza.

"Mmm," Lindsay moaned, despite herself, and then frowned. "I… I mean…"

"Oh don't worry about pretending to protest, dear," Kaydee murmured lowly. "Soon enough you'll be stuffed… and that's when you'll fight me. But until then, baby," she went on, "Enjoy it! Free dinner, hm?"

Throughout this encouragement, Lindsay ate the slice that continued to dangle in front of her face, and then, seeming to take the words to heart, she doggedly noshed on the next slice that wagged in her face.

And then the next. And then the next.

As she ate, Kaydee pressed tender, beringed fingers into Lindsay's belly, running up and down the knotted cords that caged her breasts and succulent gut. "How beautiful you are going to be," she said, and giggled. "A true work of art, made in my own image."

"Fuck you," Lindsay said, petulant. But she wordlessly accepted further offerings in the form of a couple fast-food tacos to break up the monotony, crunching through them like a lawnmower in tall grass.

And oh! The magic pill, along with the delicious food, was doing its work. Her stomach began to look more puffy with increased adipose, and her cheeks were a little more full. It was incredibly delightful to see, and it made Kaydee so fucking horny.

"There we are, sweetie," Kaydee moaned, and while her charge chewed, she began to finger herself tenderly. "Now let's get some more medicine in you before you start getting that acid reflux."

Accepting the inevitability of her fate, Lindsay opened her mouth. The pill was swallowed gracefully, and then Lindsay proceeded to keep chewing whatever food was presented in front of her growing fat face.

A full carton of ice cream later, her double chin was actually threatening to bear another ripple, and her stomach was beginning to form a second layer of softness at its top.

Twenty pounds down, so many more to go. Kaydee only hoped that eventually, once Lindsay grew past the point that her mindless noshing could possibly have caused, Lindsay would be…receptive to Kaydee's dark designs.

Another pill. Lindsay accepted it the moment Kaydee waved it in front of her face, not batting an eye. "I don't think I've ever eaten so much in one sitting," she confessed as her stomach rumbled. "I just can't stop being hungry for some reason. How much have I eaten so far tonight?"

"Just one pizza, love," Kaydee lied, smirking at the three large pizzas that Lindsay had destroyed. "And the tacos, of course."

"Hm," Lindsay added, after a few more voracious bites.

"Do you think you can handle more?" asked Kaydee, feeling the immense softness of Lindsay's second bubbling layer of tummy growing beneath her fingers.

Lindsay shrugged her plumpening shoulder in the prettiest casual gesture. "I guess I could stand another."

With that, Kaydee offered another 'antacid,' and then proceeded to
stuff Lindsay's face so effectively that Lindsay didn't even notice that
she'd put on a grand total of forty pounds in less than thirty minutes.

"Ugh," Lindsay moaned after cleaning up another couple pizzas.
Kaydee massaged the other woman with both hands while Lindsay
stifled a burp. "For some reason I'm still so hungry. What's in these
pills you're giving me?"

"I dunno," Kaydee lied, "Alka-seltzer or something?"

"Well stop giving me them," Lindsay insisted, and looked around
hungrily for her next bite. "I swear I've eaten a week's worth of food
but I'm still hungry for some reason."

"Oh, no reason?" Kaydee observed, and patted the now-indisputable
second roll of fat that smothered her stomach with a heavy second
layer. "Seems like you're making quite a pig of yourself, hm?"

Lindsay's face – which was rounding out so prettily – became a soft
oh as she looked at her own body.

"How… how?" she demanded, terrified at the sight in front of her.
"Wha- what?"

"I guess the gig is up," Kaydee laughed, and she body-slammed herself into Lindsay's growing body, which was now expanding outside of the ropes like a muffin trying desperately to escape a cage. "Time for your medicine, dear."

"No!" Lindsay cried, but Kaydee was too quick, and managed to shove a handful of four pills down her throat. Lindsay almost choked, and Kaydee patted her on the back.

"There there, you're okay," Kaydee insisted, pressing a hand into Lindsay's stomach and kneading it warmly. "Except for being forty pounds heavier in a minute."

"That's impossible," coughed Lindsay, but her eyes were wide as she turned to look at her body and the way it visibly gurgled, rumbled, then expanded like a loaf of bread in time-lapse. "God. Why… why do I feel…"

She coughed again, then, with worry etched across her face, she asked, terrified of the answer, "Why do I feel so… aroused?"

At this, Kaydee laughed — a huge, happy, belly-full of laughter that was the reason she called her store by that name. "You're just like me, baby," she cheered, and pressed a kiss upon Lindsay's baby-soft cheek. "You're a feedee."

And as Lindsay's eyebrows raised in question, Kaydee pressed her own massive stomach against Lindsay's smaller one, and taunted Lindsay with slow, sensuous pelvic thrusts.

"Don't you wish that your belly could be the same size as mine?" Kaydee whispered seductively, accentuating every word with further gyrations.

"No!" declared Lindsay vehemently, but her eyes betrayed her fascination. Also her heavy breathing; her bosoms were growing before Kaydee's eyes and Kaydee ran her fingers across them with the passion of a thousand suns. "No."

"I think you like it," Kaydee said saucily, thrusting a pill between Lindsay's lips before the other woman could protest, and then as suddenly as she began her deviant behavior, she turned around and flounced away. Happily, she had installed slanted ceiling mirrors to be able to see Lindsay's reactions even when she was turned away, and she flushed at the way Lindsay ogled her bare, naked ass.

Ninety pounds. Still the woman was fighting! It was hot, but tiresome.

She decided to take herself for a little break, to refresh herself and force an orgasm out of her too-tight body. Also to replenish her energy with a large pizza, consumed rapidly without enjoyment. This was fuel, not for pleasure.

Finally, feeling better, she came back into the room. Kaydee was pleased to hear Lindsay's stomach rumbling, and she offered the woman one more pill.

"So what will it be: more food? Or just medicine?" Kaydee crooned, wiping one hand across Lindsay's blossoming bosoms and nearly swooning at the way the massive globes gave under her fingers.

"You smell like sex," Lindsay observed, neutral in tone. "You're getting off on this."

Kaydee snickered. "Damn straight, honey. You want me to give you some relief?"

"No," Lindsay said, but her face was red as a tomato. And round as one, too, thanks to that hundred pounds of weight gain. "I don't... get off... on this..."

"Suit yourself," Kaydee said, and smiled. "So you didn't answer the question. Medicine and food, or just medicine?"

Lindsay rolled her eyes. "Medicine and food, I guess. I'm still starving."

"Hardly starving, baby," Kaydee said, and ran two sensuous hands across Lindsay's lengthening panniculus. "Rather the opposite, really."

"Fine," Lindsay grumbled, and opened her mouth with a growl. "Gimme."

With one hand feeding her captive lady her tenth pill, Kaydee pressed her fingers into the tight tight space between Lindsay's gut and pelvic bone. "Time to release you from some of these bonds," Kaydee said, and added with a puckish attitude, "at least some of you."

So saying, she released the straining ropes from where they encased Lindsay's stomach, and Lindsay breathed out with a huge sigh of relief. "Thank you," Lindsay breathed, heavily. It seemed like something was churning through her mind, but she was quiet. Just thinking loudly.

Two more pills. It was better this way, than to do them one at a time. The results were far more satisfying to watch, in Kaydee's opinion. The other woman's belly was the primary source of deposit of her new pounds, other than breasts.

And then, there she was. A hundred and twenty pounds heavier, and still so many pills to go.

And still hungrier than a cavalry of men.

"So, how you feel, baby?" Kaydee asked, pressing a kiss into Lindsay's large expansive belly, which was striped with stretch marks from her massive gains of the day.

"All right," Lindsay said, her voice soft.

The two of them sat there together, Kaydee pressing her head against Lindsay's stomach, until Lindsay finally said something.

"You know, I think I would like some help with… that thing."

"What thing?" Kaydee sweetly asked, pretending not to know. Relishing the dynamic of power that she now held over Lindsay.

And then, to her immense satisfaction, Lindsay stated: "Relief?"

This was the turning point!

Thank goodness it had come!

"Oh baby," Kaydee answered, her voice cracking. "Yes, I'm happy to."

. . . .

Kaydee pushed apart Lindsay's plump labia to access the sweet wetness underneath.

"There we go," she murmured, inserting a delicious finger into the warm flesh. She looked up at Lindsay's face, and the other woman's eyes were closed, her breath catching in her throat, and she was squirming.

"Hm, do you like that?" Kaydee asked, and she pressed one heavy hand into Lindsay's burgeoning flesh. "Yes, I think you do."

"Mmm," Lindsay urged, clearly at the edge of giving in to the sensations of pleasure. "Mmmmmm."

In response, Kaydee pulled one rope edge tighter, and allowed it to snap back against Lindsay's flesh. The sound was immensely pleasing to her, as was the scent of Lindsay's urgent need becoming more prevalent around her fingers.

So, Kaydee flicked, flicked, flicked those fingers, inside, outside, all around Lindsay's wet little clit.

Lindsay's clit was like a bead, round and hard and not too squishy, but all the flesh around it gave as Kaydee massaged. The sensation was overwhelming, and Kaydee herself found the need to touch herself as her fingers were sucked forcefully into Lindsay's vaginal channel.

"God," Kaydee breathed, rubbing in and out of Lindsay's opening. "You're so wet."

"Yeah," breathed Lindsay, and her rasping gasps tickled Kaydee's sense of imagination.

Kaydee reached over to the bottle of pills and Lindsay opened her mouth, obedient and quiet. "Good girl," murmured Kaydee, and she pressed fierce kisses across Lindsay's plump cheeks. "You look so good, darling. So delicious."

"Sure," Lindsay grumbled, accepting two more pills on her tongue, "even though I'm growing into a huge lard-ass." She swallowed thoughtfully.

A hundred and sixty pounds more on this woman does her good, Kaydee contemplated with appreciation, watching the smaller woman round out so completely.

"Nonsense!" Kaydee responded, her eyes dancing and alight. "Especially because you're growing into a huge lard-ass. Every pound makes me wetter, honey."

Lindsay seemed skeptical, her mouth pursing into a frown, but Kaydee removed the binding off one curling hand.

"But don't take my word for it." So saying, Kaydee guided the prisoner's hand down into her own private place, hefting her largesse out of the way to permit entry, and Lindsay's face began to color.

"That's what you do to me, sugarplum," Kaydee explained, and guided Lindsay's thumb firmly across her clit. "This… is… all… your… fault…"

With that, Kaydee's climax arrived, and she moaned aloud, gushing juices down her pillowlike legs with fervor.

"Oooh," Kaydee declared, shivering into the sensation. "Girl, you make me so hot."

After a few frenzied moments of finger-fucking, Kaydee opened her eyes to meet the warm, watery glow of Lindsay's eyes.

"You… you smell good," Lindsay said, as if she couldn't believe it.

"Really?" Kaydee panted, rolling her head back but trying not to close her eyes.

"Yeah," Lindsay said, with some growing confidence. "Would you… untie me a little?"

Kaydee did not indulge foolishness, and her resulting glare did not suggest otherwise, so Lindsay amended, "Just so I can get on my knees, for you?"

The heat rushed to her clit, and Kaydee nearly felt faint with desire.

"No funny business," she admonished, and then proceeded to pull out her box-cutter keychain and fulfilled the request.

At this point, Kaydee observed Lindsay sink to the ground with a sigh of relief, but the girl was earnest in her intentions. Kaydee gently parted her labia and permitted Lindsay's soft, wet, pink tongue to flirt mercilessly there.

The sensation was better than she could have imagined, and she'd imagined this kind of experience quite a lot. Her legs were weak not only from the time she'd spent standing (and exhausting her over-taxed muscles) but also from weakness in her spirit. She knew - she knew this wasn't real, it wasn't because Lindsay really liked her, but

she figured she could at least enjoy it, even if Lindsay was just trying
to find a way to escape. She just had to be the smarter one.

Not that she felt all that mentally agile, the more she watched Lindsay
lick and suck. The girl's overbloated stomach hosted two pretty
dollops of creamy breast flesh upon it, occasionally visible under the
shadow of her own massive stomach. These bobbed and flounced
like a Portuguese Man O'War floating on the ocean's surface, as
squishy and appetizing as jelly.

"Oh God," Kaydee cried as she gushed again, feeling almost as if she
were voiding her bladder with the quantity of her excess. "This is the
life."

And without any irony, Lindsay asked between licks, "So, you like
it… when I get bigger...hm?"

"Hmmmmgh," affirmed Kaydee with conviction. "I do!"

"Then how about we do our best at that," Lindsay suggested, her
voice muffled beneath Kaydee's heavy stomach.

 Kaydee smirked, not quite believing what she was hearing. "At
what?"

"Getting me bigger, silly." Lindsay's voice was low and throaty, and Kaydee felt absolutely destroyed.

"Oh hell yes," Kaydee groaned, and thrust her hand at the remaining bottle of pills. "How much did you weigh yesterday, sweetie?"

"I was hovering around two-hundred and fifty," Lindsay responded, smiling shyly yet proudly.

Kaydee inhaled noisily. "Oh god. I bet you're past four hundred pounds today... No, I'm certain of it. Can we go check?"

Lindsay nodded in assent. "Of course, darling."

They made their way to the bathroom together, giggling excitedly, both at the prospect of Lindsay's growth, and the playful yet sensuous poke Kaydee gave to Lindsay's voluminous rump.

They entered the bathroom and Lindsay nervously stepped atop the scale.

The robotic voice announced aloud, in its neutral and vaguely cheerful tone: "Four hundred and fifty one pounds."

Kaydee shuddered, a smile growing on her face. "Baby. You're at four hundred and fifty pounds!"

Lindsay bit her lip, heat pooling in her stomach. Seeing these figures that she wouldn't have been able to fathom just a few days ago was disconcerting, but she couldn't deny that she felt proud, not to mention turned on at the way Kaydee was staring at her breasts and tummy.

Kaydee came close and circled her slowly, eyes alight with appreciation, not missing a single curve. She thought to herself, "Ohhhhh, I am going to have so much fun with this girl. My girl. Lindsay is everything I ever wanted."

. . . .

Lindsay laid atop the bed, groaning. Kaydee had just fed her an entire Thai feast. Tom Kha Gai, Chicken Satay, Pad Thai, Massaman curry. Nothing had escaped her mouth, Kaydee had made sure of that- including a few dozen more special pills. "How on earth did all of that fit inside me?" she beseeched her lover.

Kaydee snickered. "Where there's a will, there's a way, my sweet. And it helps that you are such a very, very good girl. Now. Let's go see how much you've grown."

As Lindsay could no longer fit her way into the tiny bathroom,

Kaydee brought the scale into the bedroom and helped heft her lover to her feet and move onto it. The scale made a worrisome groaning noise as it sank heavily into the carpet under Lindsay's massive body, clearly hitting the maximum weight it was able to withstand.

"Six hundred and fifty pounds," the scale's robotic voice announced, crackling under the weight.

Kaydee felt herself gush within a split second of hearing the number, then ran her finger down Lindsay's face. "Well my love…. it looks like before the next time we weigh you, we might need to invest in a veterinary scale," she teased, before bringing her lips to Lindsay's hungrily. She pushed her back onto the bed roughly, ignoring the abrupt cracking sound coming from the wooden frame. Bed shopping could wait--making love to her rotund girlfriend couldn't.

Before joining Lindsay, Kaydee grabbed the bottle of pills. There were only a few left, but she was going to put every single one to good use. She started by placing one in her mouth, then kissing Lindsay again. They shared it, tongues swirling together as the tablet slowly melted. They both swallowed then Kaydee grabbed another, placing it over her clit then hovering over Lindsay's face.

"Eat it. Eat ME," she commanded, hissing sharply as Lindsay complied before she could even finish her sentence. Kaydee screamed as Lindsay swallowed both the pill and her cum.

Lindsay smirked as an idea came to her, then shoved two or three pills inside of Kaydee's pussy before diving in facefirst, slurping and sucking until she was sure she'd retrieved every trace. Kaydee screamed and shook, all the blood in her body moving to her nether regions, feeling as if she might pass out at any moment.

"My turn," Kaydee crooned when the ability to speak came back to her. She placed the last pill on Lindsay's navel and licked all around it until Lindsay was begging for release--and then a bit longer. Finally, she moved down and licked, nibbled, and sucked like she never had before.

Lindsay made noises Kaydee had never heard before as she moved between sucking her nipples, massaging every roll on her body, and going back to her pussy again and again. She kept on until Lindsay was too tired to do more than whimper when Kaydee touched her sensitive spots.

Then they both collapsed on the bed that was beginning to resemble an overturned nest for its brokenness, sated and exhausted.

But as they fell deeply asleep, Kaydee could swear she heard Lindsay murmur, "Love you, babe," as they were drifting off.

Perhaps life would start to be a little better now. Now, that they had each other.

52

ABOUT THE AUTHOR

Molly Weisser is a BBW in her own right brimming with self-love and positive sexual energy that she seeks to spread throughout the world. Her books have an international following that extends across every major continent. She lives in a major city on the east coast of the United States, and enjoys a kinky, fat-positive, polyamorous lifestyle. She enjoys large people of all genders and sexual predispositions, and especially enjoys cuddles.

She believes in Health at Every Size and tries to straddle the real-life complicated experience of being a hard-wired feedism kinkster while also wanting to be a happy and healthy plus-size person. She enjoys writing fanfiction, watching movies, and spending time with her girlfriend.

You can find out more about her ongoing and upcoming works on her Facebook page: https://www.facebook.com/MollyBBW/

For a list of her other publications available for purchase, please check out her author page on Amazon:
http://www.amazon.com/author/mollyweisser

She also maintains a presence of Patreon:
https://www.patreon.com/mollyweisser/